10

HUNGRY RABBITS

COUNTING & COLOR CONCEPTS

By Anita Lobel

Alfred A. Knopf
New York

Mama Rabbit was sad.
"I have nothing to put in my soup
pot for dinner,"
she sighed.

"But, Mama," whined ten
little rabbits.
"We are very, very, VERY
HUNGRY!"

"There is the garden,"
said Papa Rabbit.
"You are sure to find good things
for Mama's soup pot there."

Ten little rabbits agreed,
and off they hopped.

1 *ONE*

The first rabbit found ONE big PURPLE cabbage.

2 *TWO*

The second rabbit pulled up TWO WHITE onions.

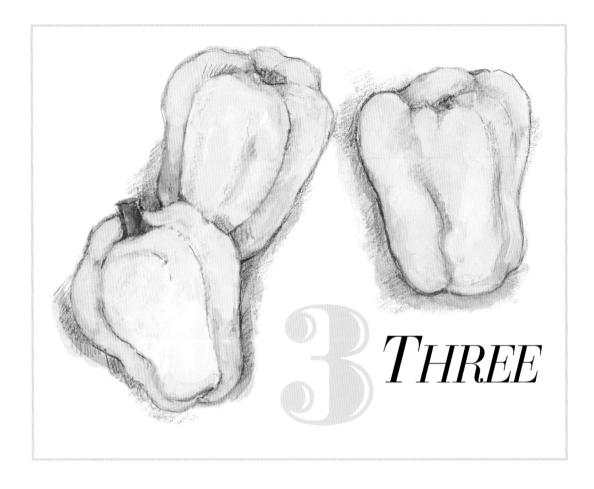

3 *THREE*

The third rabbit broke off THREE YELLOW peppers.

4 FOUR

The fourth rabbit picked FOUR RED tomatoes.

5 *FIVE*

The fifth rabbit dug up FIVE PINK potatoes.

6 *SIX*

The sixth rabbit yanked up SIX ORANGE carrots.

7 SEVEN

The seventh rabbit spotted SEVEN BROWN mushrooms.

8 *EIGHT*

The eighth rabbit gathered EIGHT BLUEBERRIES.

9 *NINE*

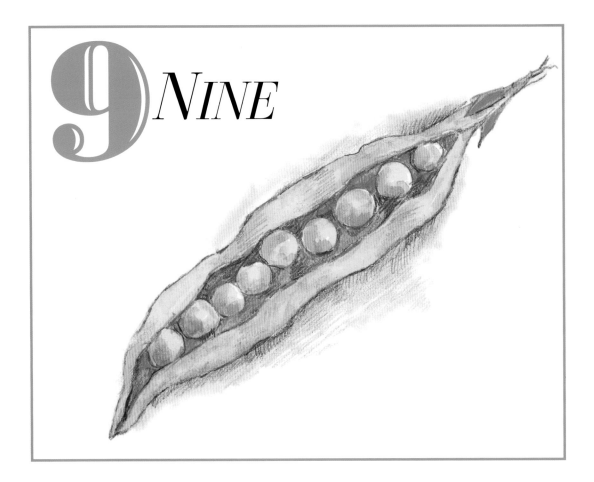

The ninth rabbit saw **NINE** GREEN peas in a pod.

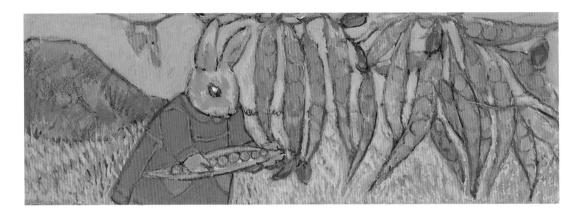

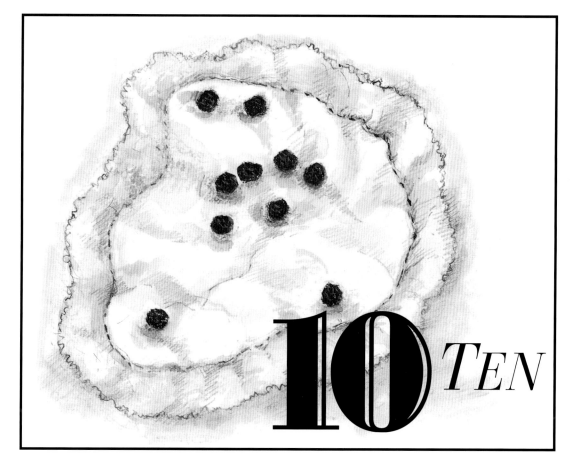

10 *TEN*

The tenth rabbit remembered
the TEN **BLACK** peppercorns in his pocket.

"Here comes dinner!"
cried ten hungry little rabbits.

"What nice rabbits we have," said Mama.
"What strong rabbits they are," said Papa.

Papa Rabbit sliced vegetables.
Ten hungry rabbits waited.

Mama Rabbit cooked soup.
Ten hungry rabbits waited.

The Rabbit family sat down to bowls
of delicious vegetable soup. Yum!

The happy rabbits were hungry no more.

THIS IS A BORZOI BOOK PUBLISHED BY ALFRED A. KNOPF

Copyright © 2012 by Anita Lobel

All rights reserved. Published in the United States by
Alfred A. Knopf, an imprint of Random House Children's Books,
a division of Random House, Inc., New York.

Knopf, Borzoi Books, and the colophon are registered trademarks of
Random House, Inc.

Visit us on the Web! www.randomhouse.com/kids

Educators and librarians, for a variety of teaching tools, visit us at
www.randomhouse.com/teachers

Library of Congress Cataloging-in-Publication Data
Lobel, Anita.
10 hungry rabbits : counting and color concepts / by Anita Lobel. — 1st ed.
p.   cm.
Summary: Ten little rabbits are hungry for supper but Mama Rabbit has nothing
to put in her soup pot, so Papa sends them to the garden where they discover
increasing numbers of foods in many different colors.
ISBN 978-0-375-86864-1 (trade) — ISBN 978-0-375-96864-8 (lib. bdg.)
[1. Rabbits—Fiction. 2. Gardens—Fiction. 3. Hunger—Fiction. 4. Counting. 5. Color.]
I. Title.
PZ7.L7794Aaf 2012
[E]—dc22
2011003514
The illustrations in this book were created using gouache and watercolor.

MANUFACTURED IN MALAYSIA
February 2012
10 9 8 7 6 5 4 3 2 1

First Edition